Second Grade—
Friends Again!

If you liked Second Grade—Friends Again! *be sure to look for this other story about Jacob:*

Second-Grade Friends
by Miriam Cohen

Second Grade—Friends Again!

by Miriam Cohen
Illustrated by Diane Palmisciano

A
LITTLE APPLE
PAPERBACK

SCHOLASTIC INC.
New York   Toronto   London   Auckland   Sydney

A LUCAS • EVANS BOOK

"When the Red Red Robin Goes Bob Bob Bobbin' Along,"
by Harry Woods, used with permission
of Bourne Music and Calicoon Music.

ISBN 0-590-45906-6

12 11 10 9 8 7 6 5 4 3 2 1   4 5 6 7 8 9/9

Printed in the U.S.A.   40

First Scholastic printing, March 1994

·Contents·

·One·

Jacob and Honey

"**M**y goodness!" Jacob's mother said. "Look at Toby. Flea time is here already."

Jacob's dog, Toby, was scratching his neck and thumping with his paw on the kitchen floor.

"Toby looks like he's playing the violin in my school orchestra," said Jacob.

Toby looked embarrassed, and he stopped scratching.

Jacob stirred his cereal around and around. Then he stirred it backwards. He thought, Toby is a bus for fleas. The fleas get on and ride around till they come to our good carpet. Then they jump off. But some fleas like to keep riding around to take a trip.

"Dear, would you get a can of flea spray today?" said Jacob's mother to his father.

"No!" cried Jacob. "You can't use flea spray because it will hurt the ozone!" Then Jacob added, "The ozone is the good stuff in the air on top of the earth." Jacob's class was studying how to save the earth. Signs all around the second grade room said, "Make the Earth Happy. Don't Pollute!" and "Save the Animals *Right* Now!"

Jacob began eating his toast like a beaver — lots of little crunches with his front teeth. Jacob was very interested in beavers. He read books about them. Then he said, "We've got to take care of the earth. Nathan says, 'Without the earth, you wouldn't have anything,' and Nathan is the smartest kid in second grade."

"It's 8:45! Hurry, Jacob! You don't want to be late for school." His mother hugged him. "Have a good day."

"Save water!" said Jacob. Then he told his dad, "Bye, Dad! Don't drink and drive!"

Jacob ran fast down the street to school. He liked to come early so he'd have plenty of time with Gregory and Franky before the bell. They weren't there yet, so he sat on a bench in the playground to wait.

"When the red, red robin comes
bob-bob-bobbin' along.
Along."

It was Honey, singing on her way to school. Honey was the biggest, roundest, and strongest kid in second grade. She was Jacob's friend. She was everybody's friend in second grade, because she always tried to help people.

"I'm just a kid again,
doin' what I did again,
singing a song!!

3

...Live, love, laugh and be happy!
When the red, red robin
comes bob-bob-bobbin' along!"

That was Honey's favorite song. Second grade sang it in mixed chorus.

When Jacob and Honey first met in kindergarten, Honey wanted to put Jacob in the doll-buggy and take care of him. It was embarrassing, but Jacob was used to it by now.

"Hi, Jacob! Hi!" called Honey, waving to him. Jacob moved over so Honey could sit on the bench. She was holding a big, sugar-coated jelly doughnut. "Here, you can have it," she said. "I don't want it because I already had one with my breakfast."

"No, thanks," said Jacob. "I'm full."

Honey was swinging her legs and looking around. She forgot she didn't want the doughnut, and started to eat it. Pretty soon, her mouth had a white sugar circle

around it, and her nose was dipped in red jelly. She was talking to Jacob and eating, but when she turned around, the bench was empty. Jacob had run to meet Gregory and Franky.

"Hey, Jacob! Did you do your homework?" they asked him.

Everybody in Mrs. Rosebloom's class was supposed to make up a slogan about saving the earth.

"Well, I didn't think of one yet," said Jacob. But then he thought, "Wait a minute. I just did! 'Don't Pollute or You'll Get a Boot!'" Jacob really liked his slogan.

Franky said, "I don't know, man. Maybe you better think up something else."

"It *could* say, 'You Better Not Pollute, or You'll Get a Boot!'" said Jacob. But Franky and Gregory didn't think that would help.

They could see Katy and Suzy in the other part of the playground, playing,

6

"Pretty Little Girls on Jaybird Street."

> *"All the pretty girls are*
> *rockin' and a rollin',*
> *slappin' and a snappin',"*

they sang. Then they slapped each other's hands, faster and faster,

> *"Criss-cross applesauce!"*

LaToya and LaTanya's father let them out of his car by the gate. "Give me some sugar," he said in a nice rumbly voice. He bent over so LaToya could kiss him on one cheek while LaTanya kissed him on the other. Then they ran to play with Suzy and Katy.

"C'mon. Let's go talk in our private place," Franky said. And Jacob, Gregory, and Franky went in the back of the bushes.

"What should we talk about?" said Jacob.

"Well . . ." Gregory started thinking, "we could talk about — umm, uhh — "

Just then, two fifth-graders, John Feeney and Alvin Jones, came and stood by the bushes. They didn't see Franky, Jacob, and Gregory.

"They're mean kids," whispered Jacob.

"They're big, too," Gregory whispered back.

"Hey!" John Feeney said, pointing at Honey. "Look at that fat kid on the bench! If she fell off, she'd crack the cement."

"She must be a baby elephant!" laughed Alvin Jones as they walked away. "I hope she never falls on me!"

Jacob, Gregory, and Franky looked at each other. Why would anybody say things like that? There *was* a lot of Honey. But she was sort of like a jelly doughnut — round and sweet, with a really good filling inside.

"You shouldn't call people fat even if they are." Gregory was shaking his head.

But Franky laughed, "A baby elephant! That's funny!"

Jacob laughed, too, until he saw that Honey was looking at them through the bushes. Jacob nudged Franky, but Franky said, "She didn't hear. See, she's smiling."

Just then, the bell rang.

"I bet I can beat you to our room!" Franky shouted.

Franky did beat Jacob and Gregory to the second-grade classroom. But that was because Jacob didn't race. He liked coming into the school and looking at everything. He liked seeing the slippery-shiny floors that Mr. Jenkins, the custodian, had polished. He always looked at everybody's drawings, and paintings, and science projects in the halls.

Fourth grade's project was hanging outside their room. Jacob stopped to look at it.

63% of our class bought
chocolate popsicles.
37% bought vanilla popsicles.

What did the two O's with a line between them mean? Why didn't anybody get a creamsicle? Jacob wondered.

It was nice knowing that Mrs. Rosebloom would greet each of them as they came in the door. "Well, good morning, Jacob! How are you today, Franky? What cute skirts you're wearing, LaToya and LaTanya!" She always sounded as if it was such a nice surprise to see her class every morning.

As Jacob sat down, he saw Nathan almost walk by their room. Nathan was busy reading his library book so he could take out another one at library period. Almost every day he took out another book.

Franky pulled him in the door. "Hey, Nathan! You better stop reading so many books. You'll get so smart your brain might bust."

As soon as they were all in their seats, Katy and Suzy started patting and fixing LaToya's and LaTanya's hair. Every day it was different. Today, their hair was in three soft puffs instead of pigtails. There was one puff on top and one on each side. Shiny red-and-blue glass balls on elastics made the puffs stay the right way.

Mrs. Rosebloom called, "Roomhelpers, please pass out the cushions for discussion time."

"Honey is sitting on two cushions, and I haven't got any," complained Suzy.

"There are plenty of cushions, Suzy," said Mrs. Rosebloom.

Jacob didn't want to, but he started remembering what happened on the playground. He knew it wasn't good to laugh at Honey, but it wasn't his fault. If she wasn't so big, those boys wouldn't have said that, and then he wouldn't have laughed. It was the big boys' fault! Jacob felt better.

"Now," Mrs. Rosebloom said, "you know we are working on ideas for Earth Day. The school is making a giant poster, and second grade is going to contribute to it. Who has thought of some slogans that tell us how to take care of the earth and to be good to it? You say it, and I'll write it on this big sheet of paper."

"We made up one together," said LaToya and LaTanya. "Hug the Earth. Don't Bug the Earth."

"What does that mean?" some of the kids asked.

"It means, don't aggravate the earth," said LaToya. "Like, if you go to the store with your brother," said LaTanya, "and you want him to get you something, and he says, 'Mama didn't say you could have that. Don't bug me, now.'"

"Oh, yes! I see," said Mrs. Rosebloom. "Well, we could think about it. I really love the first part, though. We'll surely use that.

"Jacob, have you got one for us?"

Jacob shook his head. "I *almost* have one. I just need to work on it."

Honey whispered to Suzy and Katy, "Is this any good? 'Hug the Whales'?"

Suzy and Katy told Honey they didn't know if you *could* do that, so Honey didn't say it.

Nathan put his hand up. "Don't Be

Prejudiced to Other People. Don't Hate," he said.

"No," Suzy told him. "You have to say it about the earth, *not* about people."

But Nathan said, "It *is* about the earth because people live on the earth."

"Nathan has a very good point," said Mrs. Rosebloom. They talked about it, and everyone agreed that their slogans could be about people, too.

"Hah!" cried Jacob. "That gives me a great idea!"

"What is it?" the kids asked.

"Hate Hate!" said Jacob.

"Hate Hate?" Mrs. Rosebloom tried saying it different ways. "I'm not sure. It *might* get people a little mixed up."

"But if you say that, it means you are hating, and you shouldn't hate," said Katy. "You shouldn't be prejudiced."

Jacob began to worry a little. Was laughing at somebody for being fat the same as being prejudiced?

-Two-

Trouble in Left Field

Jacob's mom and dad could hear Jacob yelling in the shower.

"Garbage Is Rotten! Don't Kill! Stop Drips! Just Say, 'Yes I Won't!' " Jacob was trying out slogans for the giant Earth Day poster. He was yelling because slogans have exclamation points, and that's what exclamation points make you do. But none of his slogans sounded right. "Boy, is it lucky I'm good at baseball," Jacob told himself when he was drying off.

"Jacob, hurry!" his father called from

15

the breakfast table. "The Whizzes are playing the Rovers!" His dad was watching a replay of last night's game on the little TV in the kitchen. The New York Whizzes was the name of the team they wanted to win.

"How's it going at third base?" his dad asked during the commercial. Jacob played baseball at school, too.

"I *used* to be third base," said Jacob. "But Mr. Zito said I was a natural left fielder, so he changed me."

"A natural left fielder," said Jacob to himself while he was eating his toast. That's what the sports announcers, Bill and Biff on TV, always said. "Wow! That Chip Goodman is a natural. Look at him hit that ball! Holy cow!"

Jacob was putting all the raisins from his cereal in a circle around his bowl. The raisins got too wet and fat from the milk, but Toby liked them. "How're your fleas, Toby?" Jacob asked. Jacob's mom had bought Toby flea powder made out of a certain kind of grass. The fleas didn't like that smell.

Then Jacob took his spoon and flipped a raisin into the air. Toby always caught the raisin, no matter how high it went.

"Ja-cob!" came a voice from the back-yard. Jacob grabbed his jacket and books.

"Don't forget your lunch," his mother said.

"Gregory's waiting for me. See ya!" he

shouted, and the kitchen door banged shut behind him. Gregory was Jacob's best friend. They walked to school together almost every day.

"Hurry up, Gregory! We have to practice some good ol' baseball." And they ran all the way to the playground.

LaToya and LaTanya were already there. They were teaching Suzy and Katy to jump rope Double Dutch. LaToya and Katy turned two ropes very fast. LaTanya jumped in the middle. Then she had to jump over both ropes and touch her shoe at the same time.

> *"Shake and bake*
> *Your boyfriend's name is Jake*
> *If you do not touch your shoe*
> *Out goes Y-O-U!"*

Honey sat and watched. She laughed and clapped when the twins' feet tapped fast like rain.

The girls stopped to rest.

"Your skirts are so cute," Katy told LaToya and LaTanya. The twins were wearing little jean skirts over their tights.

"Your sweater is cute, too," the twins told Katy. Katy's sweater had a pink fuzzy poodle on the front.

Franky and Jacob and Gregory were practicing baseball for gym. Of course, their team wasn't like the Whizzes, because girls played, too. Just for now, Jacob was pitcher.

"Smoke it over home plate, Jacob, ol' boy!" Franky grabbed the bat as if he were going to chop down a giant tree.

Jacob really wished he didn't have to stay right in front of Franky while he was pitching.

"C'mon! What are you waiting for?!" Franky shouted.

Jacob threw the ball way up and put his arms on top of his head.

"Str-r-rike!!" called Gregory.

"Strike? You're crazy!" cried Franky.

"Jacob's not supposed to throw it up in the sky someplace!"

"But I'm not *supposed* to be a pitcher. Mr. Zito said I'm a natural left fielder." Jacob said.

Franky was disgusted. He threw the bat down and walked away, shaking his head. Lucky for Jacob, the bell rang.

When it was time for gym that afternoon, Mr. Zito divided second grade into two teams. "Okay, second grade Whizzes! Let's get out there and show what we can do!" He walked out on the baseball field swinging the bats in his big brown hands.

Jacob ran out of the gym with the boys. The girls came after them. Jacob started running the way baseball men do. They jog out on the field looking serious. Then they look up and smile and wave at the cheering crowds.

"Buzz Buntley!"

"Yaay!!"

"Jacob Johnson!"

"Yaay!!"

Jacob trotted out to left field. The sky was full of ozone. The grass smelled green and juicy-sweet when he stomped on it. "My good luck is coming," Jacob said to himself.

LaToya stood on the pitcher's mound. She began snapping the ball to Gregory, who caught it almost every time. Suzy and Katy practiced sliding into first base. Honey went to her place in right field. She waved and smiled at Jacob. Then she began singing:

"When the red, red robin comes bob-bob-bobbin' along!"

LaTanya waved to her sister from second base. "Put it right here!" And LaToya did. The ball went into LaTanya's hands like a bird flying straight into the nest.

Nathan came up to bat.

"Batter-batter-batter!" hollered Franky from first base. He was trying to make Nathan nervous.

But Nathan told him, "I've got my concentration. I don't even hear you, Franky."

Mr. Zito had told them how real athletes put their minds on one thing and keep out all the rest. That was called concentration.

When the ball came over home plate, Nathan just stepped up and hit it. Then he ran toward first base. The ball went high over LaTanya's head, too high for her to reach. Jacob was hoping the ball wouldn't decide to come to left field! But it did.

"Concentrate," Jacob said to himself. "Concentrate."

"When the red, red robin comes bob-bob-bobbin' along,"

Honey sang.

"Oh, no!" the kids cried. "It's going to Jacob! He'll never get it!" Jacob was concentrating so hard the ball whizzed right by. Nathan strolled to home base and started to read his book.

Mr. Zito came out on the field to talk to Jacob. "What happened, son?"

Jacob looked at his sneakers.

"Listen, Jacob — I changed you from third base so you would have a chance to show what you can do in left field. The balls don't come out here so much. But you need to try a little harder. Okay?" Mr. Zito patted him on the shoulder.

Jacob stood alone out in left field. He stubbed his toe in the dirt and whispered, "Maybe if Honey didn't keep singing all the time — probably that's what took away my concentration."

·Three·

Honey's Big Problem

When Jacob came into the room the next morning, everybody was saying, "Eeeyew! Don't look, Jacob! Mrs. Rosebloom has a skeleton!"

"It's true!" Gregory showed Jacob. "There he is!"

Next to Mrs. Rosebloom's desk there really was a plastic skeleton man. He had part of his skin on and part off. That was so you could see what was inside a person.

"Maybe he got hit by a car, and his skin came off," Honey said.

25

"Now, we all want to know how to keep ourselves healthy, don't we?" said Mrs. Rosebloom.

"Yeeees," answered her class.

"We're going to learn about our bodies. Then we can take care of ourselves, and not be sick."

Mrs. Rosebloom showed them the plastic man's heart, and told them how it worked. She lifted the side of his head off to show his brain. Everybody knew that a brain thinks.

"But your heart is the most important part," Jacob said.

"No," said Nathan. "Your brain is, because your brain learns things for you and it tells you what to do."

Everybody began talking. They all wanted to tell what the most important part of a person was.

Mrs. Rosebloom held up her hand, "What about the food we eat? Isn't *that* important?" Then she explained how you should eat a lot of whole wheat, and fruits, and vegetables. "I know we love cookies, and candy, and treats. But are they really good for us? You know, sweets give you cavities, and they can even make you hypcractive."

Nobody said anything. They just looked at each other.

"What about birthday cakes?" Honey asked. She sounded really worried.

"Of course, we will always have birthday cakes, and candy, and sodas," Mrs. Rosebloom smiled. "How could we celebrate without them? But if you have treats every day, it wouldn't be a treat, would it?"

Honey felt the bumps in her lunch bag where the two little round apple pies were. She smiled to herself.

"Crickle, crackle, crickle," the principal's voice started coming out of the loudspeaker. "Mrs. Rosebloom's class will go to the nurse for their health checkups at this time."

"Line up, please! Nathan, will you lead the class to the nurse's office?"

"I *know* I grew a lot this year," said Gregory to Jacob as they lined up.

"I got thicker," Jacob said. He knew he wasn't any taller.

"Don't run," Mrs. Rosebloom called after them. So Suzy, Katy, LaToya and LaTanya started skipping down the hall. Honey skipped behind them, out of breath and smiling.

Mrs. Riley, the school nurse, was waiting. "My, aren't you second-graders getting big! Gracious! What is it you've been eating? Plenty of Irish potatoes, I'll bet."

The nurse's office was very white and smelled like Band-Aids.

"Me first!" Franky made muscles on both of his arms.

"All right, then, Franky. Let's see how much you weigh," Mrs. Riley said. She slid the little silver barrel over on top of the scale. Then she slid it over more. "My, Franky, you *are* big and strong," she said.

"That's because I'm from Puerto Rico," Franky told her.

Nathan and Gregory weighed exactly the same. "That's so lucky I can't believe it!" they said, and they kept shaking each other's hands.

While Honey was waiting to get weighed, Mrs. Riley asked her, "Honey, what did you have for breakfast?"

"Pancakes and syrup and . . . two jelly doughnuts, and a banana with Captain Krinkles," said Honey.

"Well, dear, you look like you've put on some weight since last time. I think I will need to talk to your mother about putting you on a little diet."

Honey's face turned red. She was embarrassed.

Suzy whispered in Honey's ear, "Go on tiptoes when you're on the scale." And LaToya and LaTanya told her, "Stand real soft. And don't breathe." But when Honey got on the scale, Mrs. Riley pushed the little barrel much farther over than she pushed it for anyone else.

When they got back to their room, everybody was telling Mrs. Rosebloom what they weighed and how tall they had grown. Jacob just told how much he weighed. Honey was very quiet.

Mrs. Rosebloom usually noticed if someone was sad. But today she was in too much of a hurry. She looked at her watch. "It's time for mixed chorus. We'll just have to skip math today. Hurry, or we'll be late!" Mrs. Rosebloom quickly led her class to the music room.

Mixed chorus was called that because second-, third-, and fourth-graders all sang together. Everybody sat in rows, and watched Mrs. Bing in front at the piano. Mrs. Bing was a large lady. She could play with one hand, and wave a pencil to lead them with the other.

Jacob whispered to Gregory, "I hope she doesn't get fussed today." It was very easy for Mrs. Bing to get fussed.

"Are we ready to open our mouths and sing like the birds?"

The mixed chorus shouted, "Yes, Mrs. Bing!"

"Away we go!"

They always warmed up with "Row, Row, Row, Your Boat," and "If You're Happy and You Know It, Clap Your Hands."

Franky did funny things when they were singing. Sometimes he opened his mouth extra wide, and sang without any sound. Sometimes he just made funny faces. Jacob and all the other boys admired him a lot. Now he was "rowing the boat" so hard he fell off his seat. That *really* fussed Mrs. Bing.

"I couldn't help it!" Franky smiled at the mixed chorus, while Mrs. Bing said what she thought about the way Franky was behaving.

Next they sang in French. It was easy. You just said, *"Fray-rah, Jock-a, Fray-rah, Jock-a. Door-may-voo?"* And somehow that meant, *"Brother Jack, brother Jack, are you sleeping?"*

Jacob was singing away. Then he noticed that Honey was quiet. Jacob thought, she always loves to sing. Maybe she feels bad about weighing so much. But I can't help it. Anyhow, she keeps bothering me when I'm trying to play baseball — always smiling and waving. How do they expect me to concentrate?

·Four·

Jacob's Losing Streak

"**P**izza today!" Everybody rushed down the steps to the cafeteria.

"Pizza! Pizza! I love you!" Franky cried.

The kids who brought their lunches in brown paper bags sat down at the big tables. The others ran to be first in line where the cafeteria ladies served the hot food. The ladies' faces were shiny with smiles under their white caps. They really liked hungry kids. "Here's a nice crispy piecc," one of them said to Jacob.

After they got their fruit cup and a carton of milk, Jacob and Gregory carried their trays to the boys' table. Franky, Nathan, and some other boys were there already. Franky was waving his pizza in the air, taking giant bites, and talking to all his friends at once. As soon as they put their trays down, Jacob and Gregory began talking, too.

That's what a cafeteria was — lots of talking and noise. There was the sound of pizza crusts crunching, sandwiches being unwrapped, and the lettuce being taken out, somebody throwing a paper at the trash can and missing, and laughing, and running to pick it up, and somebody chasing and being chased.

Lunchtime was so loud that a person could be quiet right in the middle of it, like Katy at the girls' table. She was folding the slice of ham from her sandwich over and over till it got littler and littler. Sometimes she took a tiny nibble, but mostly she was just folding and dreaming.

LaToya and LaTanya were clapping, "Pretty Little Girls on Jaybird Street," with one hand and eating their sandwiches with the other.

Honey spread all her lunch out on the table so she could decide what she was going to eat first. Mrs. Rosebloom came and leaned over Honey. She talked to her for a minute. Then she put her arm around Honey, and they walked out of the cafeteria.

Katy heard what Mrs. Rosebloom said. She told the other girls, and the girls rushed to the boys' table. "Honey has to have a diet and not eat anything that could make her fat because the fat isn't good for her health. Mrs. Rosebloom is going to call her mother. I think she was crying a little," Katy said.

"No she wasn't, she was just sad," said Suzy.

When they heard that, everybody started to think what Honey could do. Franky said, "They have those little mini-munch doughnuts at Doughnut World. She should eat those. Or," he patted his stomach, "I could eat her lunch *for* her. Yummy."

Gregory had an idea. "She could eat those little skinny pretzel sticks instead of the fat round kind!"

Franky said, "Every time she starts to eat a cookie or something fat, her mother could blow a whistle."

But Nathan said, "Fat people have a right to be fat, and skinny people have a right to be skinny. It's the United States law."

Jacob hoped Honey wouldn't be too sad. He was sorry about her trouble, but it was really her own fault. Besides, she was making him miss a lot of balls at baseball practice these days.

"C'mon!" cried Franky. "Mr. Zito has playground duty, and he said he'd practice with us at lunchtime."

Kids gobbled their lunches or threw them in the trash basket, and ran outside to the playground.

"Batter up!" called Mr. Zito. It was Suzy's turn to bat. Out in left field, Jacob waited with his legs way apart. He held both hands like a cup to be ready for the ball. Honey came back from talking to Mrs. Rosebloom, and Jacob saw her smiling at him from right field.

On first base, Franky danced around.

"C'mon, let's go!" Then he waved his hands toward Suzy. "Woo! Woo! I'm doing magic on you!"

"Mr. Zito! He's trying to make me miss!" Suzy gave Franky a very bad look through her glasses.

LaToya was pitching. She stood very still for a minute, holding the ball up in front of her, and looking at Suzy. Then she threw the ball straight and fast right over home plate. *Crack!* went Suzy's bat.

Like a great big white moon, turning over and over, that ball came down from the sky right for Jacob. Jacob dug his feet hard into the earth, held his hands very steady, and shut his eyes tight.

"Run, Jacob! Don't just stand there. Catch the ball!" everybody shouted. But Jacob's feet felt stuck to the ground. Besides, how could he see where he was running with his eyes closed?

When he opened them, Suzy's team was screaming, "Go, Suzy, go!" And Suzy

was racing from first base to second, to third, and home. Jacob chased the ball, but it was like the Gingerbread Boy. It kept on running away from him.

Jacob's team howled at him, "Jacob, look at what you did! We'll never win now! Butterfingers!"

"What happened, Jacob?" Mr. Zito put his arm around Jacob's shoulder. "Didn't you see the ball coming?"

How could he tell Mr. Zito that was just the trouble. He *did* see the ball, and he knew it was going to smack into him and send him to the hospital for an operation!

Walking back to class, Gregory stayed with Jacob. Everybody else ran ahead saying, "Jacob made us lose. He was just standing there!"

"In left field," Jacob said, "you could get hit on the head, or your arm, or anyplace. You could be out for the whole season."

"Maybe Mr. Zito would let you be the catcher," said Gregory. "That way, you wouldn't have to run." But Jacob didn't think he really wanted to be right in front of LaToya's straight eye and whizzer arm.

"I think I might have a losing streak," Jacob said.

·Five·

Strike Three!
You're Out, Jacob!

*G*arbage Is Rotten! Stop It! Jacob wrote. Then he tried *Don't Do It!* instead of *Stop It!*

"That's nice, Jacob." Honey was looking over his shoulder. She said that about everybody's work.

"Jacob," Mrs. Rosebloom said, "why don't you take a rest from working on your slogan? It will come to you when you're not even thinking about it. Work on your baseball book instead."

Every morning, second grade did

"writing proccss." That meant you could write about anything you liked, and make a book out of it. It could be a story, or it could be true. You didn't have to worry about spelling. You just spelled the word like it sounded. After you did the writing, your friends or the teacher helped you fix it, and that was called "editing."

Jacob liked it best when you got published. That was when Mrs. Rosebloom put clear, shiny plastic over your book and a pocket in the back with the check-out card. It went on the library shelf, and kids could really take your book out at library period.

Jacob loved to take out his own books. On the cover it said,

"Author, Jacob Johnson
Illustrator, Jacob Johnson."

The dedication said,

"This book is dedicated to
my best friend, Gregory Applefeld."

Gregory dedicated his books to

"My best friend, Jacob Johnson."

Jacob was halfway through his story about a boy who was a natural in baseball. He took it out of his desk, crunched it all together, and threw it in the wastebasket.

"Why did you do that?" Gregory asked him.

"I'm tired of working on it," Jacob said. "It's a dumb story anyway."

Mrs. Rosebloom held up her hand. "Class, stop what you're doing, and listen to LaToya and LaTanya's story. They really did such a good job!"

The twins came to the front of the room. They looked embarrassed. But they really wanted to read their book to the class.

"You go first." "No, you read first," they poked each other. Then they took turns reading.

"Once upon a time, three little girls lived in their apartment house on Martin Luther King Avenue. One was named Denise. One was named Crystal. They were sisters. Their friend's name was Maria. Denise had curly hair, and Crystal had curly hair, too. Maria's hair was straight in a pony tail."

Suzy told them, "You could say, 'They both had curly hair.' That way you could save work."

"That's very good editing, Suzy," Mrs. Rosebloom said.

"Every day they went down in the elevator, and played Double Dutch in the playground. But some Bad Big Boys always came, and chased them away."

"So, finally they had an idea to do a trick on those boys. Denise said,

47

'I bet you can't jump as fast as me.' "

" 'Ha Ha! I can beat you any-time,' said the worst Bad Boy. He jumped in. Then Denise and Crystal turned the ropes so fast that the boy was getting all slapped up. He was crying, 'Let me go.' They jumped him right out of the playground. He ran down Martin Luther King Avenue. He never came back to their playground again.
THE END."

Franky wasn't listening. He was roaming around in back of the room. "Hey!" he cried. "Sammy is dead!"

Mrs. Rosebloom and all the kids rushed to the Animal Corner. Cuddles, the guinea pig, and Sammy, the snake, lived there. Sammy's house had a privacy curtain. He didn't come out except when somebody reached in and dragged him.

But now he lay in his front yard, too straight and stiff.

"Oh, it's so sad. Poor Sammy," the kids said.

The guinea pig hid in his oatmeal box, watching with round shiny eyes like two brown marbles. Katy said, "Cuddles misses Sammy."

"What happened to him?" everybody wanted to know.

"Maybe he had heart trouble? Our grampa did, and he died," LaToya and LaTanya said.

"Remember how I used to put him on my arm for a bracelet?" said Honey. "He was cute."

Jacob said to Gregory, "I don't think he was cute. I like things with ears, like a dog. Snakes have no legs or anything. Yech!"

"He can't help it if he wasn't a dog." Suzy touched Sammy softly with her fingers. And Nathan said, "He had a right to be a snake. If he was ugly or anything, it doesn't matter."

"We can bury him in the playground," cried Franky. Mrs. Rosebloom gave the aluminum foil from around the celery in her lunch to wrap Sammy in.

"He looks beautiful," the kids said.

Then Franky and Nathan slowly walked Sammy out to the playground. LaToya, LaTanya, and Katy scratched a hole near the tree and patted the dirt on top of him. "Now he'll always be near kids," Franky said.

"Somebody should faint," LaToya said. "At our great-aunt's funeral, two people fainted," said LaTanya.

But Mrs. Rosebloom told them, "We all tried to take good care of Sammy when he was with us. I don't think he'd want us to be too sad. We can remember him by always being kind to our animals."

"We could get a stone and dig Sammy's name on it with a knife," said Franky. But Mrs. Rosebloom said, "Back to our classroom, and math!"

So Jacob had to listen while Mrs. Rosebloom explained "Take Away." He practiced crossing his eyes till he saw two Mrs. Roseblooms standing over him.

"Jacob, I do *not* appreciate your doing that when I am teaching."

Jacob started thinking about the accidents that could happen to you from baseball.

On the New York Whizzes, the baseball men were tall, and slow, and strong. The pitcher chewed something in his cheek. Sometimes he spit. He stood for a while, thinking what kind of ball he was going to throw. Then he did it, faster than lightning and bullets, right at the batter. Even if he ducked, the batter could get his thumb smashed. Sometimes, two men running could hit together like a car crash.

"Math is over, Jacob," said Gregory. "It's time for baseball practice."

The class followed Mr. Zito out to the ball field.

Franky told the kids, "You have to warm up your muscles." He and Gregory threw the ball really hard to each other.

"You want to warm up your muscles with me, Jacob?" said Honey.

"No, because I'm practicing my batting." Jacob swung the bat so hard he went all the way around in a circle.

"Okay! Batter up! Nathan, you're first," said Mr. Zito.

Nathan put down his library book, picked up the bat, and stepped up to home plate. He looked very serious like when he was working on a math problem.

"Put some mustard on it!" LaTanya called to LaToya, who was pitching. The ball came right to Nathan's bat, and bounced off. Nathan hurried to first base.

"Safe!" cried Mr. Zito.

Suzy hit a double. Now Nathan was on third base, and Suzy was on second. It was Jacob's turn to bat.

"Come on, Jacob! Bring Nathan home!"

Jacob grabbed the bat hard with both hands. He raised it high.

"Jacob is swatting a fly," laughed Franky.

"I am not! I think I might be getting a fever, though." Jacob felt his forehead. Then he bent over to shoo every speck of dust off home plate. He didn't want to trip over anything when he hit that ball.

Franky shouted, "C'mon! Let's get the show on the road!"

LaToya threw the ball, and Jacob ducked.

"Strike one!"

"I can't see so good today. There's

spots like baseballs in front of my eyes," Jacob said.

"Oh, yeah," said Suzy.

Jacob decided to start batting before LaToya could throw the ball.

"Strike two!"

Suddenly Jacob got a terrible picture in his mind—LaToya had hit him with the ball, and he cracked open like Plastic Man! All his muscles and eyeballs showed. The kids looked inside him and Nathan pointed, "That's his liver."

"Strike three! You're out, Jacob!"

Jacob felt so embarrassed. He couldn't look at anybody.

Honey stood up big and wide at the plate. She waved and smiled at the kids. LaToya wound up her pitching arm and let go. The ball came straight over home plate.

"Good pitch!" called Mr. Zito.

Honey whomped the ball up into the sky and over the fence. Everybody

cheered. Everybody except Jacob.

Nathan and Suzy raced home. Honey skipped, puffing and smiling, around the bases. When she got to home plate, everybody began screaming and hugging, and jumping on her. Jacob stared hard at a bump on the ground.

"Our side is the best! We won! We won!"

Kids were pushing Jacob out of the way so they could get near Honey. It was like the World Series on TV when the Whizzes won.

Franky cried, "You're so good! You're a Chocolate Chunky with raisins! I have to eat you!" and he pretended he was eating Honey's arm.

Honey smiled and smiled. She waved at Jacob. He stood by himself on the side feeling sad. Then he felt mad. He walked up to Honey and whispered, "baby elephant," right in her ear.

· Six ·

You Have to Be Happy
to Sing

Gregory hadn't come that morning to pick up Jacob. "He must be sick," Jacob said to his mom. So Jacob and Franky were sitting on the playground bench, waiting for school to begin.

"Here comes Honey," said Franky. Jacob didn't look. He kept his head down.

"Hey, Honey! Are you going to hit another homer today?!" Franky called. Honey didn't answer.

"She's not singing. I wonder why?"

Franky said to Jacob. Then he said, "Maybe Honey *shouldn't* go on a diet? If she got little and skinny, she might not bat so good."

When Honey came near, Jacob went on his hands and knees and ducked down under the bench. "Look at this ant! This ant is interesting," he called up to Franky.

"Why?" Franky asked.

"Well—if it was a black widow spider, we'd be dead in a second," said Jacob.

He waited till Honey had gone by. Then he crawled out from under the bench. Sideways, he could see Honey watching the girls jump rope. Usually she'd be laughing and clapping, but she was just standing there.

Everybody except Jacob ran to talk to Honey about yesterday. LaToya and LaTanya showed Honey how to do a high-five. That meant you slapped hands in a certain way. "All the baseball stars do that when they hit a homer," they told her.

"Honey's a hero!" Franky smacked her on the back.

"You mean a heroine, because she's a girl hero," Nathan said.

"Oh, what a cute lunchbox," Suzy and Katy told Honey. Honey's mother had bought her a Betsy Ballerina lunchbox, so she would feel better about her diet. "I was going to get a Betsy Ballerina lunchbox, but I decided to get a Batwoman one instead," Suzy said.

But Honey wasn't really listening to the kids. She was looking at Jacob. Her eyes looked like Toby's when you stepped on him by mistake, and he didn't understand why you hurt him.

Jacob looked away. Then he saw Gregory. "Hey, Gregory, where were you?" Jacob ran to meet his friend.

"Oh, I was busy."

"Busy? Busy doing what?" Jacob asked.

"I don't know."

Jacob was really puzzled. This wasn't like Gregory. He wanted to ask him, "What's the matter?" but Gregory hurried into school.

All morning, Jacob sat at his desk looking at Gregory's back. Gregory was always turning around to see what Jacob was doing. But he didn't do it once. Jacob muttered to himself, "What do I care? Everybody in the whole second grade is crazy. All they do is say, 'Honey's great! Honey's great!' And now Gregory is mad at me. Well, he can't be *my* friend *anymore*!"

Jacob wished it was time for music. He would just sing and sing and not think about any bad things. When the clock said eleven, Jacob ran to line up. Ever since kindergarten, he and Gregory always walked together. But Gregory was walking with Nathan.

When they marched into the music

room, Gregory picked the seat between Nathan and Franky. All the good seats were taken so Jacob had to sit by himself in the last row. Mrs. Bing was ready at the piano with her pencil raised. "Off we go!" she said.

Mrs. Bing waved the pencil so everybody would follow it and keep in rhythm. But Jacob couldn't help looking at her chins. They shook happily every time she hit the piano keys. Whenever Gregory slept over at Jacob's, they imitated her. They made each other fall on the floor laughing. But now Gregory wouldn't even look at Jacob.

Katy and Suzy played with Katy's long-haired purple troll on her lap, where Mrs. Bing couldn't see. Franky tickled the back of LaTanya's neck with a little feather.

After "If You're Happy and You Know It," Gregory raised his hand. "Could I go to the bathroom?"

"If you're *sure* you *really* have to," Mrs. Bing said.

In a little while, Jacob raised his hand.

"Jacob, your musical education will only suffer if you don't give it your complete attention," Mrs. Bing said. "You may go."

Gregory was washing his hands. He saw Jacob in the mirror. Jacob did an imitation of Mrs. Bing waving her pencil, but Gregory didn't even smile.

"Why are you mad?" Jacob asked.

"You know."

"No, I don't!" said Jacob.

"I heard you say Honey was a baby elephant."

Jacob cried, "I *didn't* say Honey was a baby elephant! I said . . . 'baby telephone'!" But Gregory was already going out the door.

When Jacob came into the room and saw Honey, he moaned to himself, "Why did she ever have to come to *this* school?

If only she went to another school instead, I wouldn't be having all this trouble. It's *her* fault!"

Mrs. Bing was thumping into "Fray-rah Jock-a," Jacob's favorite. The kids opened their mouths like capital O's and sang high and loud. They were happy to hear such good sounds coming out of themselves. That's why it was fun to sing. Only, Jacob just couldn't do it. You have to be happy to sing.

That night, after supper, Jacob's mom and dad were in the living room, practicing their dance steps for the PTA show. They were going to be Fred Astaire and Ginger Rogers. Jacob lay on the sofa.

"Ginger always did it with her hand out like this. It was so pretty," said Jacob's mom.

"I know, but you're sticking me with your fingernails," Jacob's dad said.

"Jacob, you look sad," his mom said.

"Did something happen at school?" Then she said, "Come on, dance with me."

Jacob got embarrassed when his mom danced with him. But he really liked it. He would kick and jump, holding onto her hands. They always laughed so much that they had to stop. But now, he just had no kicks in his legs. You have to feel happy to dance.

Jacob went upstairs very slowly. He wished he could take back those words that he had said to Honey. But mean words can stick on a person and really hurt their feelings.

He reached under his bed and took out his treasure box. He touched his reindeer's tooth, and looked at Mickey Mouse's autograph from Disneyland. Then he took out his best treasure. It was a teeny plastic root beer mug that he got from a gum machine when he was a little kid.

Jacob always wondered, How could it look *so* real? The foam really foamed, and

the root beer was goldy-brown with little sparkles of light bubbling in it. When it dropped out of the gum machine, instead of any of the other toys, Jacob felt so lucky.

Once, he almost gave it to his best friend, Gregory, but Gregory looked at Jacob and said, "I'll take something else." He knew how much Jacob really wanted to keep it. Jacob fell asleep thinking about Honey and holding his little plastic root beer mug tight in his hand.

·Seven·

Friends Again!

"**P**ut your tray right here, Jacob ol' boy."
Franky patted the seat next to him.
Gregory and Nathan were already sitting
at the cafeteria table. But Jacob carried his
tray over to the other side table.

From there, he saw Gregory as he
patted and scooped his mashed potatoes
with a spoon. "This is an army fort. And
the lima beans are the soldiers."

"Yeah!" Franky started shooting his
corn kernels at Gregory's lima beans.

Pretty soon, corn and beans were pinging all over. The teacher in charge of lunch came over. "I want *every* one of those picked up!"

Gregory and Franky were still laughing as they chased after each other's corn and beans.

Jacob would have liked to be in the vegetable fight, but he knew Gregory didn't want him. Jacob pretended he was reading his book about beavers, but he kept looking over at the girls' table. LaToya and LaTanya, and Suzy and Katy, and the rest of the girls were laughing and talking while they ate. That is, everybody but Honey was laughing and talking. She was watching the others eat their lunches, which had cream-filled cupcakes and baby Milky Ways.

Honey's Betsy Ballerina lunchbox had a hard-boiled egg (with a little salt shaker, just like the big one Jacob's mother used at home). It had crisp carrot sticks, and a whole wheat tuna sandwich with no-fat mayonnaise. Honey's mother tried to put in things so Honey wouldn't mind having to diet. She even made up recipes for "skinny" oatmeal cookies with raisins in a smiley face on each.

LaToya and LaTanya had their own bags of Cheezy Tato Chips. They held up each delicious chip, and looked at it before they crunched it.

"I'll trade you some chips for one of those cookies," LaToya said. "They look good even if they're healthy."

But LaTanya shook her head. "Uh-uh. You're not supposed to get her to eat fattening stuff."

"I forgot," said LaToya. Then she said, "Honey, you can have this pencil that's a souvenir from our family reunion."

LaToya and LaTanya had on T-shirts that said, *200 Years of Smiths, and Aren't We Proud!* It said that on the pencil, too.

Honey really liked the pencil. It

smelled so yellow and new and sharp. "What's a family reunion?" she asked the twins.

"That's when all your cousins, and aunts, and uncles, and grandmothers get together and have a picnic," said LaToya. And LaTanya said, "It's all your relatives from two hundred years. You talk about them, and you celebrate because you're glad you had so many relatives."

"Who wants to play baseball?" Franky said. He and Gregory ran out the cafeteria door to the playground. Jacob watched them go. Then he sighed and stood up. He walked over to the girls' table.

LaToya and LaTanya, Suzy and Katy got up to play "Pretty Little Girls on Jaybird Street." "Quick! Before the bell rings," they said, and ran outside.

Jacob sat down across the table from Honey. She stopped eating her skinny cookies.

Honey was so surprised, she almost

looked scared. Her mouth stayed open.

But Jacob didn't want to scare her. He just wanted Honey to laugh, and be his friend again. Jacob reached over and put something in front of Honey. It was the teeny, plastic root beer mug. "It's for you," Jacob said.

Then he picked up a carrot stick from Honey's lunch. She hadn't eaten any of them. "Want to see what you can do with carrot sticks?" Jacob put a carrot stick in each of his ears.

"Here's another one," Jacob held a carrot like a big man smoking a cigar. "Puff, puff," he blew the "carrot smoke" up in the air. Honey was smiling.

"Also," said Jacob, waving a carrot stick like Mrs. Bing. "You can EAT it." He chewed chop-chop-chop with his front teeth like Bugs Bunny.

Honey began to laugh. Jacob laughed, too. They were laughing all the way up the stairs to Mrs. Rosebloom's class.

After everyone was in their seats, Mrs. Rosebloom said, "We're not having science and social studies this afternoon. We're going to work on our part of the 'Protect the Earth' poster. Wednesday, we'll be marching into the auditorium and holding our part of the poster up so the whole school can see."

Mrs. Rosebloom had put a long, long piece of brown paper across the blackboard. On it, the class had already painted blue, wavy oceans, green and brown forests, snowy places, and sandy yellow parts for the deserts. Whales and cute baby seals swam in the oceans, animals climbed the trees and stood around in the forests. Little lizards ran in the deserts.

Franky wanted to put army planes flying across the whole picture. But Suzy said, "Army planes might shoot the animals."

"No, no!" cried Franky. "My fighter

planes shoot food to the animals! They don't shoot bullets!"

But nobody wanted to let Franky do army planes on their part. Everybody was very serious, because kids *could* save the world if people only listened.

"Nathan," said Mrs. Rosebloom, "I believe you're ready to put up your slogan."

Nathan nodded and went to the board. He pasted this sign over the Atlantic Ocean:

"You're a mammal.
I'm a mammal.
A three-toed sloth is a mammal.
So, Save the Mammals!
It Might Be You!"

"Very good, Nathan!" Mrs. Rosebloom started clapping. The rest of the class did, too.

Then Suzy and Katy went up to the board. They had worked together on their slogan:

"Don't Hurt the Animals' Mothers!
Their Babies Won't Get Food!"

Everybody clapped a lot. LaToya's and LaTanya's slogan said:

"Hug the Earth.
Don't Bug the Earth."

They had drawn little insects running around the edge of each word.

Franky said, "Cool!" But Suzy and Katy said, "Ecyew!" and "Ugh!"

Pretty soon, everybody's slogan was proudly showing at the front of the room.

"Jacob doesn't have one!" cried the kids.

But Jacob did have a slogan. He walked up to the poster. "This is just a plain one," he said. Then he wrote,

"Save The Earth *NOW!*"

The kids clapped for Jacob.

"Honey, are you ready, dear?" Mrs. Rosebloom asked.

Honey said, "Is this any good? 'Don't Hurt'?"

"Don't hurt what?" the kids wanted to know.

"Don't hurt anything," said Honey.

Mrs. Rosebloom told her, "That is a very kind slogan. Put it right up on our poster."

Then Jacob said to Honey, "Hold out your hand." He gave Honey a high-five.

Everybody clapped, and clapped, and clapped.

At three o'clock, Jacob and Gregory walked home together. Jacob felt so happy. He was singing as loud as the whole mixed chorus:

"Fray-rah Jock-a! Fray-rah Jock-a!"

Over on the field, the big boys' baseball team was practicing. *Crrraaack!*

Somebody had hit the ball high and far.

"Get the ball, kid!" the big boys yelled. It was coming down from the sky over the fence.

This time, instead of standing and waiting for the ball, Jacob ran, holding out his hands. This time, he didn't worry about getting cracked open, or getting sent to the hospital or anything.

Could Jacob catch the ball? Gregory held his breath. And the ball fell right into Jacob's hands, like it knew he was a natural!

About the Author

Many of Miriam Cohen's stories come from things that have happened to her in her own life. As a child, she, like Honey, was also overweight and remembers always being on a diet. Ms. Cohen, her professor husband, and their three sons (now all grown) have lived in many different places all over the world, including Texas, Afghanistan, and Brazil. She now lives with her husband in Sunnyside, New York, where she loves to visit schools, and talk and read to children — especially to second graders!